Hoppity-Gap

From the far side of the canal, carried on the breeze, came the sound of kids – was it four kids? – howling like a hunting pack. They were much closer now. As Ellie shut the lid of the suitcase, she heard the rustle of plastic behind her. She swung round and froze. In the doorway was a boy. He was older and bigger than she was, but what scared Ellie far more than his size was the collar he wore round his neck. It was the same as the one the dog was wearing, the dog she'd followed on to the wasteground. But it didn't look as though he was going to help her now.

Some more Young Lions you will enjoy

CHRIS POWLING

Hoppity-Gap

Illustrated by Maureen Bradley

Young Lions

An Imprint of HarperCollinsPublishers

First published in Great Britain by Hamish Hamilton Ltd 1988
First published in Young Lions 1989
4 6 8 10 9 7 5

Young Lions is an imprint of
HarperCollins Children's Books,
a division of HarperCollins Publishers Ltd,
77–85 Fulham Palace Road,
Hammersmith, London W6 8JB

Printed and bound in Great Britain by
HarperCollins Manufacturing, Glasgow

For Elsie

Chapter 1

COMING DOWN the street was a dog:
hoppity-gap, hoppity-gap, hoppity-gap.
Ellie saw it at once. "Quick, Joe," she
said.

Hastily, she stepped back in the
Hotel. She was frightened of dogs. They
jumped up at you and made your
clothes dirty and even bit you sometimes. "Do you hear me, Joe?" Ellie
whispered. "You must always stay
away from strange dogs."

Even this dog, though? Ellie stared at
it curiously. Oh, it was strange all right
but not at all frightening. This dog

1

made Ellie want to laugh . . . or maybe cry. For it only had three legs.

Hoppity-gap, hoppity-gap, hoppity-gap.

From the top step of the Hotel doorway, Ellie peeked round the stonework at the back leg which wasn't there: gap-hoppity, gap-hoppity, gap-hoppity. Closer and closer it came. Ellie couldn't shift her eyes from it. There was more gap than dog, somehow — a sort of emptiness propping up the rest of the animal. "Stop it, Joe," Ellie hissed. "It's rude to look at the bad bit."

So she looked at the good bits instead. There were plenty of them. The dog had perky ears, a curled-up tail and a glossy coat, all smartly brushed. "It's got bright eyes too, Joe," said Ellie softly. "And a wet nose. That means it's a healthy dog."

Joe didn't answer. He never did, of course, except when Ellie answered for him. Right now, though, she was too busy checking details about the dog — including the collar. As it passed the Hotel's main entrance, she had the clearest possible view. "It's a brand-new collar," Ellie exclaimed. "With silvery studs all round it. Somebody really loves that dog, Joe. As much as I love you, maybe."

Well, nearly. Nobody could love a dog as much as she loved Joe, Ellie was sure of that. "Who do you think it belongs to, Joe?" she asked.

Again, no reply.

Not that Ellie expected one. When your only friend is a *pretend* friend, you get used to doing all the talking. "Come on," she said suddenly. "Let's follow the dog and find out who the owner is."

4

She was so amazed at herself, she gasped out loud. Was she serious? She scowled and nodded her head before she could change her mind. "Yes, I know we ought to ask Dad first, but he's in bed, Joe. As usual, I'm supposed to keep myself amused till he gets up. That's all I ever do these days — stooge around hotels waiting for Dad. Serve him right if I have an adventure, for once. Anyway, we'll be back before he finds out. Okay?"

Joe wouldn't budge. She had to grab the air where his hand would have been and jerk him along behind her. "If we don't get a move on the dog will be out of sight," Ellie said.

It almost was. Already it was turning the corner at the far end of the street. Still dragging Joe, Ellie hurried after it. "We'll soon catch up," she said.

To her surprise, they didn't. A three-legged dog travels faster than most people realise. "What we've got to do," said Ellie, "is sort of slink along like a spy — only at top speed. Think you can manage it, Joe?"

Joe was already managing it. He hadn't much choice when Ellie was in this sort of mood.

As the dog led them further and

further from the Hotel, Ellie helped Joe across roads (always doing his kerb drill), down alleyways, under a fence or two (being careful not to snag his clothes), round the back of some shops, past a fire-station, through a small recreation ground (with swings and a roundabout they hadn't time for), and over a low brick wall.

And all the time they were *slinky*.

They had to be in the having-a-lie-in hush of Sunday morning. The loudest sound they could hear was the ding-ding-ding-ding-ding of a church bell. "That dog won't pick up *your* footsteps, Joe," Ellie remarked. "If anyone gives the game away, it'll be me."

This was true. No one ever caught Joe out. Even Dad's friends only noticed Joe when Ellie spoke up for him. "Is that your voice, Ellie?" they'd ask. "How quaint to have a friend who only says what you want him to say . . ."

Ellie hated talk like this because it reminded her Joe wasn't real. "You're real to me, Joe," she insisted. "Just as real as that hoppity-gap dog we're following. But where's it brought us? We're miles from the Hotel already. Will it go hoppity-gap, hoppity-gap all

8

the way to the horizon? This is just a wasteland, isn't it?"

Ellie could smell cats and stinging nettles. Also the sour-sweet stink of a canal. It was exactly the sort of place Dad told her to avoid. He went on and on about it. Nervously, she looked around. At least it was deserted. There was no one near enough to threaten her . . . or was there? What about over to the left where the skyline merged with the motorway? "Five kids, Joe," Ellie counted. "Tough-looking kids, too. What are they doing, I wonder?"

Stop-stop-stop-stop-stop rang the faraway bell in the steeple.

Ellie sighed and turned back the way she'd come.

Then halted.

She bit her lip. "No," she said. "I'm fed up with being *sensible*. I want an

adventure, Joe. We said we'd find out who owns this three-legged dog and that's what we're going to do. Why should those kids bother us?"

And she pushed down the barbed wire fence which blocked their way, let Joe high-step over it ahead of her, then straddled it herself.

Now they were really in the wilderness.

The grass sloped away from them, tangled and dank, down to the canal with its mud-coloured water. Was this where the dog was heading? "Hoppity-gap, hoppity-gap," said Ellie. "That dog's almost home, Joe, I bet you. How can we give up now when we're so close to finding out?"

Joe said nothing. Even a pretend-friend knows when he's wasting his breath.

Chapter 2

TWENTY YARDS from the canal, Ellie hesitated. Had she gone mad? What was she doing in this leftover stretch of city which was no use to anyone? She remembered her father's name for such a place.

The back of beyond.

He meant somewhere so ugly and out of the way no one would ever choose to live there . . . somewhere exactly like here. This was the back of beyond all right. Dad seemed a million miles away. So did everybody else in the world apart from those five kids, cocky and rumbustious, over by the railway bridge now. Were they searching for something on the track? Ellie could hear their faint wolf-like hoots echoing across the emptiness. Good job she'd got Joe with her. "What did you say, Joe?" she asked.

As usual, Joe was right — the sky *was* clouding over. Ellie sensed rain in the air as well as the staleness of the stinging nettles.

But where was the dog?

Still ahead, apparently, somewhere in the bushes. "See Joe?" she said huskily. "I told you it was almost home. If we're quick we can still get back before anyone notices us. This track must be leading somewhere — yes, it's a camp! Well . . . a sort of camp."

It was a hut, deep in the weeds, with rough tin walls and plastic sheeting for

a roof. "A bit make-shift," said Ellie.
"But I bet it's cosy inside."

It was, too.

She found the dog curled up in a basket stuffed with newspapers, next to an old, battered suitcase. These apart, the hut was empty. "Hello, dog," Ellie said. "Is this where you live? You won't jump up at me or bite me, will you? Promise? See, Joe? It's wagging its tail. We still don't know who it belongs to, though. Sorry? What did you say?"

Joe hadn't said a word. It was the dog which had spoken. That's what Ellie wanted to believe anyway. "Look in the suitcase?" she asked.

"Yes."

"Really?"

"Yes."

Deep down she knew she was speaking for him. "I'm making you talk, dog," she admitted. "Just like I make Joe talk. Right, Joe?"

"Right, Ellie."

"See?" Ellie explained to the dog. "I can twist my voice to sound like anyone I choose. I'm a born mimic, Dad says. And he should know. He's in show business, you see. He stands up on a stage and gets people laughing — well, most of the time anyway. Joe and I go on tour with him. We travel all over the country, Joe and me. We go to lots of different schools and lots of different clubs and theatres where Dad's appearing and lots of different hotels and boarding houses afterwards. It's really exciting, dog. It's really . . . really . . ."

She broke off as her eyes filled with tears. "It's really *lonely*," she said.

"Lonely?" asked the dog.

"Yes, lonely. I like being with Dad but he's so busy and tired all the time. The only real friend I've got — well, kind of real — is Joe."

"And me," replied the dog.

"Yes, I've got you now. For a little while, anyway. You're smashing. You're not one of those dirty, bitey, jumping-up type dogs at all."

"Of course not," she made Joe say. "A dirty, bitey, jumping-up type dog doesn't get given a collar like that — brand-new with silvery studs."

"That's true, Joe. So who is the owner?"

She was begining to feel better. She wiped her face on her sleeve, had a good sniff and took another look at the suitcase. "I've only got to lift the lid, Joe. Would that do any harm?"

"Why not let the dog tell you?"

"Great idea, Joe. Dog, should I look in the suitcase?"

"Go ahead," said the dog.

"Okay, so *I* said it," Ellie shrugged. "But I bet if the dog could talk, it would give the same answer. Right, Joe?"

"Right," came Joe's voice.

"So what am I waiting for?" asked Ellie.

Quickly, before she talked herself out of it, she stretched out a hand. The lid of the suitcase lifted as easy as a wink.

Inside, there was a packet of dog

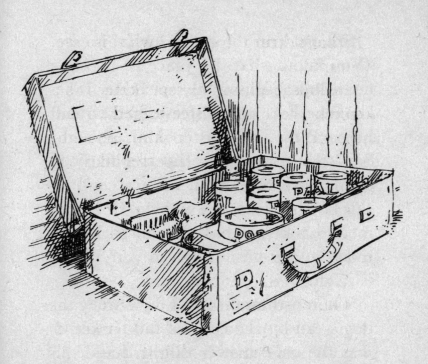

biscuits. There was a dog's bowl, too, plus six tins of dog-food, a can-opener, a huge, much-chewed marrowbone and a brush and comb for grooming. "Also there's a spare collar," Ellie exclaimed. "With silvery studs just like the one the dog's wearing."

She held up the collar for Joe to see. "You know what this place is, Joe? It's not a hut at all, strictly speaking. It's a kennel. For our three-legged friend here. Who looks after him, though? Someone must come here regularly to open these tins. Hold on a second — this bowl is clean as a whistle. Does that mean his keeper has already been here today . . . or hasn't arrived yet? Which is it, dog?"

Thump-thump-thump went the dog's tail on the edge of the basket. It was the only answer Ellie got and this time she didn't dare speak for him. His head was tilted to one side as if he were listening.

From the far side of the canal, carried on the breeze, came the sound of kids — was it four kids? — howling like a hunting pack. They were much closer now.

Ellie swallowed hard and shoved the collar back in the suitcase. "Time for us to go, Joe," she said.

"As fast as we can," Joe added.

Too late.

As Ellie shut the lid, she heard the rustle of plastic behind her. She swung round and froze. In the doorway was a boy. He was older and bigger than she was, but what scared Ellie far more than his size was the collar he wore round his neck. It was brand-new, with silvery studs.

Chapter 3

"JOE!" ELLIE YELPED.

"Joe?" said the boy. "Who's Joe?"

He knelt down to stroke the dog which barked and skittered and tail-wagged all round him the way most dogs do when a favourite person returns. "Who's Joe?" he repeated.

"He's my best friend."

"Where is he, then?"

"Close by," said Ellie.

"He'd better be."

"Why do you say that?"

"Because you need all the help you can get, kid. You're trespassing on our patch. Know what that means?"

"No."

"You've never seen a collar like this before — on a person, I mean?"

"No."

He fingered his leather necklace with its silvery studs. "We all wear them," he said. "It's a sort of uniform. The Dog Team is famous in these parts."

"The Dog Team?" said Ellie. "What's that? Is it a gang?"

"You bet it is. We've even got a special bark — yip! yip! yip!"

"I know," Ellie wailed. "I heard you just now over by the motorway. Then by the railway bridge. It sounded really creepy."

"That's the way it's supposed to sound — dead creepy — so it keeps outsiders off our territory. Outsiders like you, for instance."

"Sorry," said Ellie quickly. "We'll go straightaway if you like."

"We?"

"Me and Joe."

"Oh, yes. This friend of yours who's close by. I was forgetting him. Funny, that. I could've sworn he was here in the hut with you — thought I heard voices. Three voices. Two were from kids and one was a kind of bark like a dog."

He gave her a sideways look. "Was it you?" he asked. "Doing all three of them?"

"Yes."

"How come?"

Ellie sighed. The same old explanation every time. About her Dad. About her knack for putting on voices, just like him. About why she needed Joe. By now she'd spelled it out to scores of kids and they always reacted in the same way. 'Your Dad's in show-biz? Wow! That must be terrific!'. Did she really have to go through it once more? "It's boring," she protested.

"Tell me anyway," said the boy in the dog collar.

So she did, as quickly as she could, perched on the suitcase with her arms

round her knees, while her listener sat
with the dog in his lap, not taking his
eyes from her.

When she'd finished he gave a long,
low whistle. "Show-biz?" he said.
"Your Dad's really in show-biz?"

"Yes."

"That's ace!"

"Sometimes it is," Ellie agreed.

"And this Joe-bloke is just a pretend-
friend, right?"

Fiercely, Ellie shook her head. "He's
real enough for me. And he never lets
me down."

"Yeah?"

"Not ever."

"Glad to hear it. Must be handy,
that. What's your name, kid?"

"Ellie."

"I'm Chandu. And this dog you've
been following is called . . . Dog."

"Dog?"

Chandu nodded. "Just Dog. It's all the name he's got. What do you think of him?"

"He's lovely."

"Even if he's only got three legs?"

Ellie blinked in surprise. "What difference does that make?"

"A lot to most people. Before our gang adopted him he was a stray — just a flea-bitten bag of bones to tell the truth. Even now he needs a lot of looking after. Isn't that right, boy?"

He rolled Dog over on his back to tickle his stomach. Three legs paddled gleefully in the air — the missing leg somehow the most gleeful of all. "That's my job," Chandu said. "Looking after Dog, I mean. That's why I'm here now. I feed him and brush him and keep him fit. The rest of the gang are useless. Can't be bothered, really. They don't even like him much. Except for Red, maybe."

"Who's Red?"

"She's leader of the Dog Team. A real oddball, she is. To her Dog is magical — a sort of mascot to hold the gang together. Reckon she'd treat Dog okay if she wasn't trying to be so tough all the time. Without me, though, he's had it."

"Lucky for Dog you're around, then."

"That's the trouble. I won't be around for much longer."

"You're leaving the Dog Team?"

"Got to. Next week Mum and me are moving to a new flat across the moors. Pretty bad news for Dog, that."

"Can't you take him with you?"

"To a flat?"

"Suppose not," said Ellie. "What happens to him when you're gone, then?"

Chandu shrugged. "Oh, the gang will try to cope for a while — Red'll see to that. But they'll soon get tired of it. He'll finish up as a stray again, I expect. And you can stop looking at me like that, kid. I don't like it either. Been worried skinny about it as a matter of fact."

"But there must be something you can do."

"Like what?"

"I don't know," Ellie said.

"Exactly."

Gloomily, Chandu looked down at Dog. In the odd, creamy light that filtered through the hut's plastic roof, he looked sad enough to have said goodbye to Dog already. Ellie knew

how he felt. She'd be the same if she lost Joe. "Have you got any ideas, Joe?" she asked.

"Only one," she made Joe reply.

"What's that, Joe?"

"A new owner for Dog," answered Joe.

"Hear that, Chandu?" she asked.

Despite himself, Chandu grinned. "Brilliant," he said. "If you weren't moving your lips, I'd never guess you were talking — it's like this Joe kid is actually here!"

"What about his idea?"

"A new owner for Dog? No good, Ellie. There are loads of dogs without homes round here. Who's going to take on a three-legged mongrel?"

"Me," said Ellie quickly. "He can come back to the Hotel with us right now."

Chandu blinked in surprise. For a moment he seemed to be considering it, then, with a toss of his head, he pulled himself together. "Nah," he said. "That's stupid. It doesn't make sense. A posh kid like you adopting Dog? What will your father say?"

"He'll make a fuss to begin with but he'll give in eventually. He always does. Provided it's no bother to him and keeps me quiet, he'll agree to anything. Besides, plenty of his friends travel around with pets so why can't I?"

"You're serious?"

"Of course."

"Ellie, it won't work."

"Why not? Won't Dog settle down with us?"

"It's not that. It's just too sudden, that's all. You can't pick up a pet the instant you fancy it — like it was a bag of chips. It's ... it's a *commitment*. You've got to think hard about it first."

"I have been thinking about it," said Ellie. "I've been thinking about it for months ... except I've only just realised it. I'm tired of being on my own, Chandu, and I'm bored stiff with pretend-friends even if they never let you down. Sorry, Joe — I love you, I really do — but this is my chance to have a *real* friend for once."

"It won't be for once, kid. It'll be forever."

"I *meant* forever."

"Yes, but ... "

"But what? It won't be easy, I can see that. There are bound to be snags. How can it be worse than leaving him with the Dog Team, though?"

"It can't, I suppose."

"There you are, then. Unless ... "

"Unless what?"

Ellie paused, but not for long. Why should she hold back now? "Unless you're too *jealous* to let me have him," she said.

"Jealous?" Chandu snapped.

"Leave her alone!" came Joe's voice.

"Pick someone your own size," Dog barked.

Slowly, Chandu's fist dropped to his side. "You're unbelievable, kid," he said. "Your mouth makes the shapes, but it's their words that come out. I thought Red was weird, but you're something else . . . you really take the biscuit."

"The dog biscuit?" Ellie said.

She bent forward to scratch Dog's upside-down tummy. She was careful not to look at Chandu in case the longing in her eyes put him off completely. Why was it other kids never understood the truth about her life — about how dreary and dull it could be?

Except Joe, of course.

Joe understood.

And maybe Dog would, after this. Maybe Dog would change everything. "I really do want him," she whispered.

Chandu sat back on his heels. She

heard him take a deep breath. "Okay," he said.

She looked up at once. "You mean it? You really mean it?"

"Not much choice, is there? I'm snookered, kid. So Dog's yours . . . almost."

"Almost?"

"There's still one problem."

"What's that?"

"Them."

He jerked a thumb towards the doorway. The whoop-whoop-whoop of the Dog Team was so close now, Ellie could pick out one bark that was louder and sharper than the rest. "Is that Red?" she asked.

Chandu nodded grimly. "They're almost here. And if they catch us, Dog's had it. Red'll never give him up even if it's for his own good. Our only chance is

to sneak back to this Hotel of yours
without them seeing us . . . and believe
me that won't be easy. Wish us luck,
kid. We're going to need it."

Chapter 4

PUSHING THE SUITCASE ahead of them, they crawled through the weeds on hands and knees till they reached the first gap in the undergrowth. Here, Chandu signalled a halt. Cautiously, he lifted himself and looked back towards the hut. "Can you see them?" he hissed.

"Where?"

"The other side of the canal. By the dead tree."

That close? Ellie tightened her grip on Dog's collar and cased aside the stinging-nettles. Their hot, spidery tips brushed her skin but she forced herself to take no notice. What did a few stings matter when the Dog Team was on your trail? "Can they see us?" she whispered.

"Not yet. Keep still, though. We'll need a good start if we're going to get you and Dog back to the Hotel. Red's got the sharpest eyes of any kid I know. Especially when she's looking for Dog."

"She really loves Dog?"

"In a way, yes — a loony, Red-like way. The others couldn't care less. They only put up with him because of Red. They're afraid of her, a bit."

"Are you?"

"A bit, yes. Anyone would be. She's a spooky kid."

Ellie could see that. Even at this distance, with tall grass between them, she could pick out the mean, wrung-out expression on Red's face. The rest of the gang, two boys and a girl, looked quite normal in comparison. "What do you think of her?" Chandu asked.

"She seems sad."

"Sad?"

"Sad, yes. The others are ordinary, really — apart from the collars round their necks. Red's different."

"You bet, she is. Ajay and Charlie and Donna are as fed up with her as I am but they're too scared to break up the Dog Team. So would I be if I wasn't moving."

"Poor Red," said Ellie.

"Poor Red? Kid, you're *daft*."

Maybe Chandu had a point, Ellie thought. Feeling sorry for Red wasn't easy.

Especially right now.

Red had stiffened suddenly, like a hound that's tracked down its quarry.

Every part of her body seemed to point in their direction. "It's the suitcase," Chandu groaned. "She's seen the suitcase."

Too late to pull it back under cover. By now Ajay, Charlie and Donna had seen it as well. "Chandu?" Red called.

"Chandu?" yapped the others.

"Going somewhere, Chandu?"

"Yeah, going somewhere?"

Red's thin, edgy voice sneered across the scrubland. "Taking someone with you to this new flat across the moors, Chandu? A three-legged lodger, perhaps? The Council won't like that much . . . "

"Nah, not much . . . "

"You bet they won't . . . "

"Against Council rules, pets are . . . "

"Pets in Council flats are out of order, Chandu . . . "

"Yeah, out of order . . . "

The jeers of the Dog Team died away. For a moment there was silence. Then Red spoke again. "It's not just the Council, Chandu," she grated. "I don't like it, neither. I don't like it at all. Got an excuse for bunking off, have you? If

so I'd better hear it . . . like in the next sixty seconds."

Her words hung in the air. Above her, the sky was darkening. It had a bruised, coppery look — a look Red didn't much fancy judging by the way she glared up at it.

Chandu groaned again. "That's all we need, kid. There's a storm on its way. Red can't stand storms. Her being so jittery, they really freak her out."

"Maybe . . . maybe it's *exactly* what we need, then," said Ellie thoughtfully.

"Sorry?"

"Chandu, what's that old building down there by the water?"

"Old warehouse, I think."

"Can we get there ahead of Red?"

"Yes, if we dump the suitcase and run full pelt. What's the point of that, though?"

"Well, the Hotel's out of reach now so we've got to have a change of plan. Is Red really as nasty as you say, Chandu?"

"She's worse!"

"I'm not so sure. She reminds me of some of Dad's friends — they're tough on top, but underneath they're not tough at all. Maybe Red's like that."

"If you say so, kid. Can't see that it matters much now."

"Yes it does . . . and I know a way to find out."

"How?"

"We'll have a show-down in that old warehouse."

"A show-down?" said Chandu faintly. "With Red? Kid, you're more of a nutter than she is."

"About the same, I reckon," Ellie said.

And before he could stop her, she stood up.

Chapter 5

IT WAS the perfect place for a show-
down, no doubt about that. Red licked
her lips the instant she saw where
they'd gone. "Gottem," she said.

"You sure?" Ajay asked.

"They're skulking about inside —
take my word for it."

"Is Dog there, too?"

"Must be."

"How do you know, Red?"

"I can sniff 'em — all three of 'em.
This kid with Chandu is the start of his
new gang. They're stealing Dog for a
mascot."

Ajay, Charlie and Donna looked at each other uneasily. They'd seen Red in this sort of mood before. She'd be even worse when the storm started. Especially here, a place they'd always avoided. "Not exactly handsome, is it?" Charlie said.

"Ugly, more like," said Donna.

"Suits 'em, then," Red growled. "Suits me, too."

This place? It was hard to believe this place suited anybody. Like a repair-shed for a train or perhaps a garage for juggernaut lorries, it fronted the canal for more than a hundred yards. There wasn't a truck to be seen, though, and no trace of any rolling-stock. "What kind of dump is it?" Charlie asked.

"Warehouse," said Red. "Empty warehouse. From when this was a working canal."

"Looks in good nick, considering."

"Built to last."

"Sure to be locked up, though," Ajay objected. "How would they get in?"

"They're here," said Red shortly. "Anyone want to argue?"

"No, Red."

"No."

"No."

"Good."

Red scanned the building, taking it in: the dingy brickwork, the low-pitched roof, the tall windows with their wire-mesh protection. "They think they're safe," she said. "But they're not. Not when we've discovered where they're hiding. What they are, as they're about to find out, is *trapped*."

She spat out the last word, then broke off.

She looked up at the sky again.

The others watched her closely from the corners of their eyes. The pinched, tight expression was back on her face, the look Red always had when she was working herself up to a fit of spitefulness.

Tough luck, Chandu.

And tough luck, Chandu's new friend.

Only Dog would get away with it, as usual. Red was as easy on Dog as she was hard on everyone else. They'd seen that before, too. "Hey, it's starting to rain," Donna exclaimed.

"Starting?" said Charlie. "It's teeming down."

All round them now leaves glistened and bent under the downpour. Yet still there was no thunder, no lightning-flash, just a rat-tat-tat of raindrops they couldn't flinch from because Red wasn't flinching.

How long before she made a move? Till they were wet through?

Not quite . . .

So suddenly it made them jump, the first thunderclap split the sky from the motorway in the East to the moors in the West. At once Red jerked her head.

Yip! Yip! Yip!

54

The Dog Team was back in business. Through rain so heavy they could barely see each other, they raced towards the hazy outline of the warehouse. "In here," Red called.

How she'd spotted it they'd never
know — the gap in the brickwork
wasn't even door-size. Maybe she
smelled it. They were too busy scram-
bling inside to ask her. At least she'd
got them out of the weather.

Or out of the feel of it, anyway. The
sound was even worse spread across
acres of roof. On either side of them,
stretching off into the gloom as far as
they could see, were shelves and racks
and bays, all empty. In their throats
was the taste of dust and dead air which
always fills abandoned buildings.
"Where do we go now?" Ajay said.
"Which direction, I mean?"

"Both directions."

"We separate, Red?"

"Two against two?" added Donna in
alarm.

"Only till we find them. Then it's *four* against two."

"But they could be anywhere, Red. This place is crammed with hidey-holes. It'll take hours."

"That so, Charlie? Got somethin'
you'd rather be doin'?"

"No."

"What's the problem, then?"

"No problem, Red."

"Thought you'd say that. You stay
with me . . . Ajay, you go with Donna.
Give us a howl if you find 'em. We'll do
the same. Got it?"

"Sure, Red."

"And don't let them get away . . .
either of them. But that kid, whoever
she is, most of all. Right?"

"Right," said Ajay. "Er . . . Red?"

"Yes?"

"You feeling okay?"

"What?"

"You seem sort of . . . pale. Your
face, I mean. Thought you might've
picked up a chill or something out there
in the rain. Anyone might, Red. It's

only natural getting a chill in this weather."

Red was drenched, certainly. That was obvious from her slicked-down hair to her sopping-wet plimsolls. But so were the rest of them. It was her flushed cheeks and the wild glint in her eyes that was worrying. Ajay didn't want to mention this. Probably he'd said too much already. "You tryin' to tell me something?" Red snarled.

"No, Red."

"Good."

"Glad we've got that sorted out," said Donna. "Now let's get on with it, shall we? This place gives me goosepimples."

"Me too," said Charlie.

"And me," Ajay admitted.

Also Red from the way she looked. Why was she dithering? Was she actually . . .

" . . . scared?" said Ajay.

"Me?"

Ajay hesitated. "Them," he said at last. "I meant Chandu and this kid he's teamed up with. Reckon they're scared, Red?"

"Wouldn't you be?"

"Reckon I would," said Ajay. "Reckon it's scary here for *anybody*."

"Including me?"

"Anybody," Ajay repeated.

Slowly Red flicked the rain, if it was rain, from her forehead. "So I'm scared, am I?" she said. "That what you're sayin'?"

Ajay shrugged and took a step backwards. "Yeah," he said at last. "Maybe I am."

"Like that, is it?"

"Like that," Ajay said.

63

Now it was out in the open, they were almost relieved. The fight had been a long time coming. Red lifted her hands edge-on, karate-style, while Ajay bunched his fists. Both half-crouched as they started to circle each other, shuffling up dust with every step. What stopped them in their tracks was the sound of Red's name, short and sharp.

It echoed from the warehouse rafters more like a bark than a word. "Red!"

She froze. "What was — "

"Red!"

"Dog?" Ajay breathed.

"Red!"

Was it really Dog? Calling Red's name? What kind of dog could do that? Red's colour was ghost-like now. "It's . . . it's got to be Chandu," she said hoarsely.

"Chandu?" said Donna. "Since when has Chandu done dog impressions?"

"It's that kid, then."

"Red!" came the bark again.

"Look!" Charlie gasped.

Hoppity-gap, hoppity-gap, hoppity-gap.

Down the central aisle of the warehouse pattered Dog. He sat down just out of their reach, his mouth moving

up-and-down as if he were crunching a
dog biscuit . . . or as if he were speaking. "Red," he yapped. "It's all over.
The Dog Team's finished, can't you see
that? Give up the gang, Red."

"It's Chandu," Red repeated. "Or that kid."

"It's not," said Chandu. "See?"

He stepped out from behind some shelving, Ellie by his side. "Leave them alone, Red," said Dog. "All of them. Who needs the Dog Team?"

"He's talking," gasped Charlie. "Dog's actually talking. The words are coming out of his mouth."

"That's impossible," Ajay stammered. "I don't believe it."

"I do," said Donna. "This weird blinkin' place is turning us all into nutcases. I've had enough. Red, you can keep your manky Dog Team. And your manky dog-collar. Load of rubbish, anyway. Don't need Dog to tell me that."

"Wait — " Red began.

"Wait for what?" demanded Charlie.

67

"Donna's right. This gang is the pits. Been wanting to say that for a long time. I'm off, Red. And don't try to stop me."

His hands were trembling, and so were Donna's, as they unbuckled their collars. "Wait," Red begged.

"Here," said Ajay. "You can have mine, as well."

And a third collar clattered on the warehouse floor as he and Charlie and Donna backed away. At the gap in the brickwork they swung round together and hustled their way through in a flurry of kicks and elbowing. Their voices were lost in the rain.

Red didn't move.

Her gaze was on the pile of collars. "It was you, kid," she said.

"Me?" said Ellie.

"*You* wrecked the Dog Team, right?

It was you all along. You want Dog for yourself, it's obvious. You can't con me like the rest of them. Make Dog talk now — while I'm watching you."

Her eyes, fixed on Ellie, were full of hate. "It's not her," yapped Dog. "What gives you that idea? The Dog Team should've split up long ago. You just couldn't see it, Red."

Red's mouth gaped open. Not for a single bark had Ellie's lips even twitched. Not one bark. Slowly, Red turned towards Dog. "It's . . . it's really you?" she whispered.

"See for yourself."

"And you want to go off with this kid?"

"You bet."

Red's face was suddenly blank. Without another word she loosened her own collar, bent down, and laid it carefully beside the others. As she ducked through the gap she glanced back at Dog once, her breath hissing through her teeth. The sound was as tiny as it could be against the commotion of the storm outside, but Ellie didn't miss it.

"Goodbye, Red!" barked Dog.

"And good riddance," said Chandu.

But he was still careful to check the landscape for any sign of her. "She's gone," he said at last. "Wow! I've never seen Red in such a state. She was really spooked!"

"She was really crying, too," said Ellie.

Chapter 6

CHANDU SAID goodbye at the barbed-wire fence between the back of beyond and the rest of the city. "You were amazing, Ellie," he said. "Just amazing. Even *I* thought Dog was talking!"

"It's easy when your Dad's a ventriloquist," said Ellie.

"Can he really throw his voice anywhere?"

"Anywhere he likes. And any voice, too. Dad's really good — he's had years of practice. I'm still learning."

"Still learning?" Chandu exclaimed. "Strikes me you're perfect already.

Why didn't you tell me from the start you could talk without moving your lips?"

"She's shy," explained Dog.

"Didn't want you to think she was a show-off," Joe added.

"See what I mean?" Chandu laughed. "Fantastic! So was giving Dog a biscuit to make his mouth move. Stroke of genius, that."

"Good enough to beat Red, anyway," said Ellie.

"Serve her right," Chandu snorted.

"Think so?"

"Don't you?"

Ellie was looking back across the wasteland. It didn't seem so dangerous now the sun was coming out. The canal was quite friendly in a way and far off towards the motorway the long line of the warehouse had a neat, almost welcoming look. Funny how fast things can change . . .

"What does your watch say, Chandu?" she asked.

"Twelve o'clock. Dead on."

"That's when Dad gets up on a Sunday," said Ellie. "The crack of noon, he calls it. We've got to go."

"Bet he's a great bloke," said Chandu. "Bet it's terrific having a Dad in show-biz — "

He broke off remembering what she'd said in the hut. "Well, it'll be terrific from now on," he said. "With Dog for company."

"You bet," said Ellie. "Goodbye, Chandu. Don't suppose we'll ever meet again."

"Reckon not. On the other hand you won't be meeting Red, either! Goodbye, Joe-and-Ellie. Been nice knowing you."

"Cheers, Chandu," said Joe. "Hope you're happy in your new flat across the moors."

"'Bye, Chandu," barked Dog.

"'Bye, Dog," said Chandu gruffly.

"Ellie, you will see he's okay, won't you? You won't let me down . . . you'll do what's best for him?"

"You know I will."

"Promise?"

"I promise."

"And you'll stay away from places like this? You were lucky today, you know."

"I know," said Ellie, with a shiver. "Never again, Chandu."

"Suppose that's it, then."

"Suppose it is, yes."

They grinned at each other, suddenly awkward.

"Kid," Chandu said. "You may be posh but you're all right."

He was still waving when Ellie lost sight of him beyond the low brick wall round the recreation ground. "No time for a go on that roundabout," she said.

"Or the swings, I'm afraid. Sorry, Joe. Another day, perhaps."

"Fine," said Joe.

"How about you, Dog?"

"Yip-yip-yip," said Dog.

"Hey," said Ellie. "That wasn't me. You did that."

"Yip-yip-yip!"

Wagging his curled-up tail, Dog frisked along beside her: hoppity-gap, hoppity-gap, hoppity-gap. Ellie beamed with delight. She didn't forget Joe, though. She held his hand past the alleyways and the shops and the fire-station, and as they crawled back under the fences she made sure he didn't snag his clothes. Also, at the main roads, she insisted on helping him with his kerb-drill. "Because I still love you, Joe," she explained. "Even if I have got Dog as a pet."

"Have you?" said Joe.

"Maybe I have. I'm not really sure. What do you think, Joe?"

"Depends what's best for him, Ellie. That's what you promised Chandu."

"But what *is* best for him?"

"Why not ask Red."

"Red?"

"Come on, Ellie. Stop kidding yourself. Do you really think you've seen the last of her? She'll be waiting for us at the Hotel, I expect."

"Yes?"

"Bound to be."

And that's exactly where Red was. Ellie saw her at once, huddled in the Hotel entrance. "Right again, Joe," she murmured. "You always are."

Red mooched down the steps as they approached, her hair still spiky from the rain. "Guessed this was where

you'd be staying," she said. "Only
place in the city swish enough for someone like you. Don't worry, kid. I'm not
here to duff you up. Wanted to say a
proper goodbye to Dog, that's all."

"I know," said Ellie.

"Do you?"

"You love Dog," Ellie said. "I could tell that the first time I saw you. Probably you'd have looked after him as well as Chandu if you weren't so busy trying to be tough."

"You reckon?"

Red bent down to fondle Dog. Without her collar and away from the wasteland, she wasn't the same person — except for the tight, pinched expression on her face. "Yeah, well," she said. "Too late to think about that now. Nifty trick you played back there, kid. What with the storm as well you really gave me the heeby-jeebies. Took me a while to tumble it. You're a ventriloquist, right?"

"Right."

"Seen one of them on the telly."

"Probably my Dad," Ellie said.

"On the telly?"

"Lots of times."

"Hear that, Dog?" said Red. "You really got lucky. This kid has a star in the family. It'll be fantastic living with her."

"Fantastic," said Ellie.

Well, wouldn't it? Fantastic hotels and boarding houses to stay in, fantastic hours backstage while Dad prepared his act or rehearsed his act or performed his act, fantastic hellos and goodbyes to friends you'd never met before and maybe would never meet again . . . what a life. Really fantastic.

On the other hand it did feel fantastic some of the time. Was it *ever* like that for most kids? Be fair, Ellie. "What about you, Red?" she asked.

"Me?"

"Looking after Dog, I mean. Now you've given up that potty Dog Team you could do it properly."

"Properly?"

"Sure," said Ellie.

"Maybe I could," said Red in surprise.

"He's making a terrific fuss of you. If you ask me, that's what he's been after all along — to have you to himself."

"You reckon?"

Red squinted up at her suspiciously while Dog smothered her face with licks. "I don't get it," she said. "I thought you wanted Dog."

"I do. I've never wanted anything so much in my life. It's not up to me, though, and it's not up to you either. The choice has got to be Dog's."

"Between the two of us? You'd let Dog decide?"

"It's the only way," said Ellie.

"Yeah," Red said. "It is."

She pushed Dog away and stood up. To make it quite clear she wasn't bothered which one of them he chose, she glanced casually at the brightening, almost-blue sky. "Your vote then,

Dog," she yawned. "It's me or her. Want to stay in these parts, do you?"

Yip! Yip! Yip!

"Who said that?"

"Wasn't me, Red."

"You sure?"

Ellie shrugged. Her face was stiff as a mask. Red stared at her, not believing it. "Kid," she said thickly, "that truly was Dog's voice, was it . . . truly?"

"He picked you, Red. Definitely."

"He's mine, then," said Red.

And grabbing Dog by his brand-new, silvery-studded collar she turned away fast — but not so fast she hid the ear-to-ear grin on her face.

Ellie watched the pair of them as they scuttled along the pavement, dodging puddles, the girl in the skimpy anorak and the dog with its glossy coat, perky ears and missing leg.

Hoppity-gap, hoppity-gap, hoppity-gap.

At the corner, Red forgot to wave and Dog didn't look back. "Goodbye," Ellie called after them.

For five full minutes after they'd

disappeared, she went on standing there. She knew she must go in soon. Her famous Dad would be out of his bath by now and knocking on her door to take her to the Hotel restaurant for lunch where he was sure to be spotted, sure to be asked for autographs. It was all part of the exciting world of show-biz.

Ellie sighed. "It would never have worked, Joe," she said. "Not trekking from one hotel to another. Chandu realised that when he told us it was all

too sudden. Did I do right, though? Is Dog with his proper owner now? How about an answer for once?"

Of course, Joe didn't reply. But Ellie was half-certain that the space where his head would have been if he weren't a pretend-friend, gave a nod.

The Paddington Books

MICHAEL BOND

Paddington is a *very* rare bear indeed! He'd travelled all the way from darkest Peru (with only a jar of marmalade, a suitcase and his hat) when the Brown family first met him on Paddington Station. Since then their lives have never been quite the same . . . for things just seem to *happen* to Paddington – chaotic things.

What *other* bear could turn his friend's wedding into an uproar by getting the wedding ring stuck on his paw? Or glue himself to his dancing partner's back with his marmalade sandwich? *Only* Paddington . . . but as he says himself, 'Oh dear, I'm in trouble again.'

'Within a comparatively short time, Paddington has joined Pooh as one of the great bears of children's literature.'   *The Teacher*

Paddington's own particular brand of chaos comes up often in Young Lions – in *A Bear Called Paddington, More About Paddington, Paddington Goes to Town, Paddington Helps Out, Paddington at Large, Paddington Abroad, Paddington Takes the Air, Paddington Marches On, Paddington at Work, Paddington on Top, Paddington Takes the Test, Paddingtons Blue Peter Story Book* and *Paddington on the Screen.*

THE DEMON BIKE RIDER

Robert Leeson

There was a ghost on Barker's Bonk: a horned demon that
made a terrible howling noise as it glided along in the dusk – on
a bicycle. When Mike and his friends first heard about the
Demon Bike Rider they thought a bike-riding ghost could
only be a joke. But then one night they saw it, and heard
it, and suddenly they were running so fast there was no time
to laugh.

Other odd things keep happening. A mysterious stranger
seems to be making secret explorations of the old cottage on the
Bonk. And who on earth planted a whole lot of trees upside
down in Mr Whitehurst's garden? It is all to do with the
Demon Bike Rider, whose story is finally unravelled with as
much hilarity as haunting.